CW00847475

Disney's

Belle

Hippo

Scholastic Children's Books
Commonwealth House, 1–19 New Oxford Street,
London WC1A 1NU, UK
a division of Scholastic Ltd
London ~ New York ~ Toronto ~ Sydney ~ Auckland

First published in the UK by Scholastic Ltd, 1997

© 1996 Disney

ISBN 0 590 19451 8

Typeset by TW Typesetting, Midsomer Norton, Somerset
Printed and bound in Spain by G.Z. Printek

THE HEART'S EYES

Belle sighed as she walked down the little road to the market. Every day was the same in that quiet country town. She saw the same people and they always said the very same things.

"Hello! How are you? What a beautiful day…"

It was many years since she and her father, Maurice, had come here to live, yet she still felt like a stranger.

Belle's favourite pastime was reading.

Her dream was to own a thousand, even a million different books. Luckily, in the town there was a small library where she could borrow lots of books. She felt at home among the well-stocked book-shelves.

"Hello. I've brought back your book. Are there any new ones?" The librarian smiled.

"You were here only yesterday!" He liked Belle; she was kind and friendly, and since there weren't many people who went into the library, he rarely had anyone to talk to.

"Tell me something, Belle. Why do you like reading so much?"

"Books make me dream and they help me feel less lonely. I adore adventure stories, love stories, tales in which lots of fantastic things happen." Belle's voice was full of enthusiasm. "My mother liked to read, too. I listened to her for hours, without ever getting tired, and I could see, in my mind's eye, exactly what she was telling me."

"Then she taught me to read, and from that moment

on, books have always kept me company. She said that they help you understand things better, that they can take you to far-off lands and let you live through experiences which everyday life could never offer." The memory saddened Belle: "I think she was right."

The librarian was touched.

"Well, then, I'll give you this book as a gift; I know that it's your favourite!" Belle walked away, clutching the book. As she walked through the market, she thought back to her conversation with the librarian. It was a long time since she had talked to anyone about her mother.

Belle's mother was an extraordinary woman: intelligent, creative and bold. It was just like her to marry a penniless inventor with his head in the clouds! Belle knew that her mother had fought hard to marry Maurice. Her family was noble and rich, and her parents, who had dreamed of a very different match for her, were utterly opposed to the marriage.

But the beautiful Arlette had given up everything to be with that adorable, absent-minded, misunderstood inventor. As she grew up, Belle slowly came to under- stand her

mother's decision. Her life with Maurice had been wonderful, even if it had not been easy.

But Arlette had never given up. She chose to live with the man she loved. And then Belle had arrived. Her mother often told her about the immense happiness that her birth had brought her. She was so proud of the baby girl.

Belle reached the town square. She sat down on the edge of the fountain and opened her book. But her mind was full of thoughts. Her mother, Arlette, had died at an early age, after a long illness. Belle could still hear the lilting tones of her voice.

"I am sure that you will manage without me, Belle, but your father won't.

He needs you. Don't ever leave him. Please don't cry. Life has so much to offer you, if only you want to succeed. Remember: look with your heart's eyes, and never let yourself be fooled by appearances…"

To escape their sad memories, Belle and her father moved to a little town in the centre of France, surrounded by green hills. Life passed by, peaceful and even a bit dull, as they waited for the day when something wonderful would happen. For Maurice, an invention would one day make him rich and famous. For Belle, the love of her life, a true love, would give

her the courage to face everything and everyone, just as her mother had done.

A Strange Girl

"Hi, Belle!" Janine the shepherdess stopped at the fountain to let her sheep drink. Her friend's voice snapped her back into reality.

"Oh, Janine, I'm so happy to see you!"

"Is it interesting?" the little blonde girl asked, pointing to the book.

"It's wonderful; she is falling in love and is about to discover…"

Belle read enthusiastically while Janine listened, fascinated by her beautiful and intelligent friend. She seemed so different from the other girls in the village, even if, at times, she seemed a bit strange!

"The baker's wife said that you're very resourceful." Janine interrupted suddenly. "And Monsieur Potinç, talking to the milkman, said you were creative, too. But to me, you're adorable and I love you very

much!" she concluded, hugging her.

"I love you, too!" smiled Belle.

"But you really are a bit strange," insisted the little shepherdess. "For example, how can you not like Gaston?

He's absolutely gorgeous! All the girls in the village are in love with him. Oh, if only Gaston would take notice of me!"

"Gaston, the greatest hunter in the kingdom!" laughed Belle. "I'll explain it to you another time. Goodbye, Janine. My father is waiting for me."

But, instead, it was Gaston himself who was waiting for her, not far away, with his friend Le Fou. As she drew nearer she could not help noticing that Janine was right: he was tall, strong, handsome, but...

"Hi, Belle!" he said, grabbing the book out of her hands. "It's about time

you got these books out of your head. You and your reading: the whole town is talking about it! It's not right for girls to read; they start thinking and strange ideas get into their heads!"

How dare Gaston say that?

"Gaston, you are primordial!"

"Thank you, Belle," he said, smiling. He had no idea what that word meant.

"I was wrong," thought Belle, as she picked up her book which Gaston had tossed into the mud. "He isn't just primordial, he's also ignorant and rude."

The rumble of an explosion from the cellar where her father was working put an end to the discussion. Worried, Belle ran quickly towards home. Maurice was grappling with an invention that was giving him a lot of problems.

"I'll never make it work!"

"Oh, of course you'll make it work," Belle said encouragingly. "Tomorrow at the fair you'll win first prize!"

"Do you really think so?" replied Maurice. His daughter certainly knew how to boost his spirits.

"I'm sure of it!" said Belle, smiling, as Maurice went right back to work. But she had a peculiar feeling. She thought back to what Janine had said, and to

Gaston. "Father, do you think I'm strange?"

"Why would you think a silly thing like that?" Belle tried to confide in him. "I'm not sure I fit in here. There's no-one I can really talk to."

"What do you think of Gaston? They

say he's a handsome boy."

"He may be handsome, but he's ill-mannered and arrogant," replied Belle.

Maurice, meanwhile, had almost finished adjusting his latest invention.

"Don't you worry, Belle, because thanks to this we'll be able to change our lives completely!" He was working on a machine which chopped wood and stacked it in neat piles. One more screw, another bolt, and he would have the invention of the century – if only it worked!

"It works!" cried Maurice. The machine huffed and sputtered, moving regularly.

"You've done it!" cried Belle, hugging him. There wasn't a moment to lose.

"Saddle up Philippe, child!" And Maurice left for the fair: this was the event they had been waiting for!

Left all alone, Belle thought she

would finally be able to finish her book in peace. Instead, someone knocked on the door. Oh no, Gaston! The last person in the world she wanted to see! And why was he all dressed up, with that triumphant look on his face?

"This is the day when all your dreams will come true!" he declared, confidently, as he sat down and stretched out his legs on the table, resting his muddy boots right on top of Belle's book.

His boots left brown stains all over the precious volume. He obviously felt at home. Belle frowned.

"What on earth do you know about my dreams, Gaston?"

No, that vulgar, arrogant young man had no place in her dreams. In her future there was no rustic hunting lodge; Belle would never become a housewife who spent her life cooking wildfowl, massaging a tired hunter's feet, or bringing up six or seven little children who were as loud and stupid as their father.

"Say you'll marry me!" Gaston insisted. He was edging closer the whole time, convinced that she would throw herself into his arms. Belle backed away.

"Gaston, I ... I ... I really don't deserve you," she blurted out. He was very close now, leaning suavely against

the door as he prepared to kiss her. She had to do something quickly. Belle flung open the door wildly, and Gaston lost his balance, stumbled out and fell into the pond in front of the house! Belle shut the door with a sigh of relief.

Peeking out through the window, she was horrified to see a crowd of townspeople, who Gaston had invited to witness the wedding. Furious, the young man got up and walked away, followed by the faithful Le Fou.

"I told you that Belle would become my wife, and I'm going to marry her, one way or the other!" Belle smiled; he certainly had looked silly. Gaston, the idol of the village, loved by all the girls and envied by all the boys!

She was sure that by now everyone would have gone away, disappointed that the celebration would not be taking place after all. But, as soon as she opened the door she saw Janine, who had come after hearing that Gaston was planning to marry her best friend.

"You said no to Gaston?!" cried the shepherdess in disbelief. Little Janine would have given anything to have been in her shoes that day.

"I will never become the wife of that rude, brainless idiot. No, Janine, he is not the love of my dreams; my life will not be wasted on Gaston. I know that destiny has something else in store for me."

Jokingly, she tied a handkerchief under her chin, imitating the housewives she often met at the market.

"Why of course, my dear husband! Anything you want, my dear husband!" She laughed, amused. "How do I look? It doesn't seem the right uniform for me!"

"It's all foolishness. Anyway, you've turned down a brilliant offer: marrying the best man in the whole town!" Janine just couldn't understand her.

"It's not just a feeling, Janine. I've never told anyone this, but something happened to me a few years ago..."

THE CASTLE, THE ROSE, THE FEAR

"Just after my mother died, my father took me to a fair, which was held every year in a small town not far from where we lived. He was trying to take my mind off things, and I had never been to a fair, so I was very happy.

"We left early in the morning. It was a beautiful spring day. I was wearing my prettiest dress and we rattled along the road on the gig drawn by Philippe the horse. Father and I were really enjoying ourselves, chatting and singing our favourite songs.

"When we reached the town, I was fascinated by everything that was going on. The tree-lined streets around the square were jam-packed with people. There were gipsies, too, looking so beautiful with their dark, sparkling eyes and their colourful clothes, wandering around, jangling their bracelets and earrings.

"Everywhere there were stalls with sweets, fruit, and all kinds of things to buy. I'll never forget the table with dolls: they were made of rags, sewn by a little old woman who had lined them up in a row, with clothes that looked like real ones, and long, curly hair. They were beautiful!

"I strolled around the fair, looking at everything. There were acrobats, a band playing cheerful music, a puppet show, and an organ grinder with a naughty

little monkey. Meanwhile, my father had stopped at a stand where a strange old man was making the most beautiful crystal balls ever seen. They appeared at the end of a glass-blowing rod as if by magic. They looked just like little soap bubbles, and were so splendid, so sparkling, and so fragile, that everyone who stopped for a look stood open-mouthed in amazement.

" 'Look at all the people here!' my father said. 'And we're right next to where they are showing the inventions. Belle, we're going to have a great audience today!' That day, Father had a surprise. He had invented a 'clothes-wringer', a machine with large rollers which turned when you pulled a lever, and there was a tub to catch all the water. All you had to do was put wet clothes through the cylinders and they came out perfectly wrung and ready to go on the clothesline. The sun would do the rest. Father was sure that his invention would amaze everyone. 'Ladies and gentlemen! Come and see the most extraordinary object ever beheld! In the blink of an eye, without getting wet, and with no effort whatsoever…'

"I left my father to his work and wandered off to enjoy the festivities. In one corner of the square was an old gipsy woman. 'Come, my pretty! Come and let

me read your hand!' she
said, walking up
to me as I
passed by.

" 'No,
no, I'm not
interested,' I
stammered.
'What's that?
Don't you
want to
know your
future?
Courage,
my little

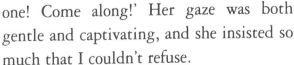

one! Come along!' Her gaze was both
gentle and captivating, and she insisted so
much that I couldn't refuse.

"The gipsy smiled at me, holding my
hand in hers. 'So, let me see. Amazing
things are waiting for you in the future,
my dear,' she began. She probably said

the same thing to everyone, I thought, as she spoke of a long and happy life, of love and riches, of desires fulfilled and dreams come true. I went along with it, of course. It all seemed like a big joke.

"All of a sudden, though, a serious expression came over her face. She frowned, and concentrated even harder. 'There's a castle in your future: a great, shining castle; and a rose, but its petals are falling, one by one, with the passing of time, like the sand in an hourglass. And then ... then...'

"Suddenly, the gipsy jumped up with a frightened look on her face, as though she had seen something terrible. 'Go away! Get out of here,' she told me harshly, letting my hand drop.

" 'What is it? What did you see?' I asked her. 'Nothing, nothing at all. Go away, now. I have things to do!' repeated the gipsy woman. But I insisted. 'I beg you, tell me what you have seen!' I convinced her to tell me.

" 'My dear, you will have to be strong enough to take on the whole world. Always do as your courageous spirit tells you,' she said, her voice returning to its peaceful and comforting tone, 'and your life will change forever. But first, you must encounter the castle, the rose and … the fear!'

"She wouldn't add any more, regardless of my pleas, and I left her, my soul shaken and confused. What could that gipsy woman have meant?"

Janine had listened, spellbound, to every word of her friend's amazing story, without daring to interrupt her. Her eyes were wide with wonder.

"Did she… did she really say all that? Oh, Belle, it's tremendous! A castle, a rose and fear! It gives me the shivers!"

Later, sitting in the field in front of her house, Belle smiled as she remembered again the gipsy's prophesy. "I'm sure that my life will change!" She picked a dandelion; immediately, a light breeze carried off its delicate seeds, scattering them about and wafting them far, far away, just like her dreams. Suddenly, a neighing made her start. Philippe, the horse, had returned. But he was alone and he was obviously terrified!

29

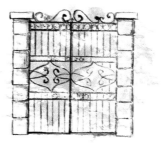

BELLE'S SACRIFICE

"Philippe? What are you doing here? Where's Father?" Something must have happened! Belle grabbed her cape and mounted the horse. They set off at a gallop. Philippe would take her to her father. They arrived at a forest, shrouded in mist. Philippe stopped in front of a castle gate, in the middle of the desolate forest. Everything was dark, deserted, gloomy and very frightening!

"What could this place be?" Belle wondered, staring around her with a lost look. Why had Philippe brought her here? She dismounted, and saw Maurice's hat, lying on the ground beyond the rusty iron fence.

"Father!" She summoned up all her courage and, walking up to the castle, pushed open the enormous door. "Is anyone home? Hello?"

Silence filled the dark entrance hall.

"Father? Father, are you here?" Belle cried, as she ran anxiously down the corridors of the castle. She had the feeling that she was being followed. Maybe it

had been foolish to wander into that terrible place, all alone. But her concern for Maurice was stronger than her fear.

She imagined finding her father lying exhausted, perhaps even injured. After bravely walking into lots of unknown rooms and climbing up many steps, Belle found him. Maurice was locked in a cold, dark, prison in one of the castle towers, half-frozen, shaking from his cough.

"There's no time to explain! You have to get out of here! Right now!" Maurice cried, terrified for her safety.

"I won't leave you!" Belle replied, forcefully. But a deep groan from behind her made her jump.

"What are you doing here?" The owner of the castle spoke out, from where he was hiding in the shadows. Belle shuddered.

"I've come for my father. I beg you, let him go. Can't you see he's sick? Take me in his place!"

"Belle, don't! You don't know what you're saying!" Maurice shouted. Belle closed her eyes: she had to follow her heart, and her heart told her that she was doing the right thing.

"You must promise to stay here forever!" was the response from the mysterious voice in the shadows. Forever!

"Come into the light!" said Belle. She had to put a face to that voice, she needed to know who she was talking to. She opened her eyes wide, then covered them at once with her arm, to escape from the awful vision before her. Was it a man? No, it was a monster! Without knowing how, she found the strength to whisper,

"You have my word." Saying this, she fell to her knees.

From her prison cell, Belle watched her father leave. She had not even had a chance to embrace him for the last time. And now she was the prisoner of that cruel, monstrous creature. Forever!

But the voice sounded less terrible

when he said,

"I will show you to your room."

So, she wasn't to be kept locked up in the prison? She followed him up the stairways of the enormous castle. The bleak atmosphere, those monstrous statues, and strangest of all, the candelabra which the Beast carried in his hand could talk!

Not even in her wildest dreams had Belle ever come across anything like it! How tall was the Beast? Eight feet? Nine? Maybe even more? He walked with heavy steps, resting on his large,

hairy paws, his back a bit hunched. His
voice was harsh yet distant, as if it came

from inside a box.

"The castle is yours now," he
announced. "You may go any-
where you please, but not into
the west wing!"

"What's in the west wing?" Belle
asked.

"It is forbidden!" The answer came in
a kind of a growl. They had arrived in
front of the door to her room, when the
Beast added:

"Tonight you will dine with me! And
this is not an invitation, it's an order!"

So, Belle found herself alone in a
strange room. Everything had happened
so quickly that she couldn't get the
events of the day straight in her mind!
Someone was knocking on the door, but
when it opened, Belle had another shock.
A talking teapot, named Mrs Potts, was

waiting outside her room.

Mrs Potts smiled at her encouragingly and offered her tea in a dainty little chipped teacup, named Chip, who was as talkative and friendly as a child! Belle discovered that a powerful spell had transformed all the servants in the castle into living, talking household objects.

So she was not surprised when the clock, who was once the butler, came to announce that dinner was being served in the dining hall.

Belle had resolved not to take dinner with her captor. She had promised to remain there, and she would remain, but she didn't want to have anything to do with him. That monster was keeping her there against her will, but he expected her to be his dinner companion! She didn't even care if she starved to death. It was snowing outside and she felt terribly alone. She wondered what her mother would have done in that situation; well, she certainly wouldn't have sat there crying uselessly!

"You'll see that the master is not so bad, once you get to know him better!" It was the wardrobe who spoke this time. By now, nothing surprised her.

"Why don't you give him a chance?" insisted the wardrobe. Belle found herself smiling. Night had fallen by the time she decided to leave her room. She was hungry, so she went to look for the kitchen.

"What a pleasure it is to see that you have changed your mind!" said Cogsworth, the butler. Lumiere, the major-domo,

who was now
the candelabra,
showed off,
giving her a
gallant kiss on
the hand. The
servants went to
work to prepare
her an excellent
meal, and every-
one begged her
to stay with them,

promising her that they would do everything possible to make her stay at the
castle pleasant.

Their warm welcome made her forget
her sadness for a moment. She was too
shaken up to sleep, so she decided to take
a tour of the castle, guided by Lumiere
and Cogsworth, of course! The butler
gaily told her everything about the
tapestries and carpets, the coats of armour

and decorations.

"What's up there?" Belle interrupted suddenly. Startled, Cogsworth stammered something about the west wing. Belle decided that she would go there, whatever might happen, for the key to the mystery was probably hidden in that forbidden place. She pretended to follow her guides, but as soon as the butler and Lumiere were distracted, she took the opportunity to sneak off.

The stairs which led to the west wing

were dark, and the walls were covered with spiders' webs. Belle pushed open a huge door and found a room so damp, stale-smelling, dirty, and full of broken furniture, shattered mirrors and torn, ragged curtains that only a monster could even think of living there!

Belle went into the devastated room. What had reduced it to this state? The fury of a wild beast, or the despair of a human being? There was a portrait hanging on the wall: it was horribly ripped, and only the eyes were still visible. They were a young man's eyes: blue, intense and beautiful. They seemed to stare at her imploringly. Where had she seen them before? And what was that soft glow coming from the darkness of the abandoned room?

A rose protected by a glass dome was resting on a table in front of the open window. Attracted by the flower, she lifted the cover and saw that a few petals had fallen. Her heart leaped in her breast: the castle, the rose and the fear!

She remembered the gipsy woman's prophecy. Suddenly Belle understood what had frightened the fortune teller. As she read Belle's palm, she had seen a vision of the Beast! She stared at the glowing rose: she wanted to touch it. She reached out her hand. But at that moment a tremendous roar echoed through the room.

THE ESCAPE

The Beast leaped through the open window and landed in the room. Belle crept back, trembling, as the enormous creature bent over the rose and covered it with the glass dome, holding it to himself like a precious treasure, as if to protect it. Belle saw the terror in his eyes. She didn't understand why he was so frightened, but that rose was certainly very important to him.

Only when he was sure that the rose was unharmed did his fear give way to rage. He smashed a table and chair against the wall, and then turned, magnificent in his anger, to Belle.

"Why have you come here?" he growled.

"I ... I'm sorry... I meant no harm," stammered the girl.

"Don't you understand what might have happened?" There was still terror in the Beast's eyes as he looked at the glowing rose, as though it represented his only chance for salvation. Then, he turned his fury on Belle.

"Go away! Get out of here!" he screamed. The girl stumbled down the stairs, her soul shaken by fear. She flew past Lumiere and Cogsworth.

"Where are you going?" the candelabra called out to her as he saw her running off.

"I'm sorry... I know I promised... but I can't stay here a minute longer!" Belle said without slowing down.

"Oh, no, wait, please, wait!" echoed the voice of the butler behind her. But she couldn't wait; she had to escape, to get far away from that place, from the rage of the Beast. Desperately, Belle crossed the park. Philippe was waiting there for her. She jumped up into the saddle and galloped away, straight into a blizzard which blinded her and made the going almost impossible. But nothing was going to stop her; she had to get away from that place. At all costs!

Belle shivered inside the cape which she had flung over her shoulders, as Philippe plunged down the snow-covered tracks

which took them deeper into the blizzard.

"Away! I have to get away, as far away

as possible from that savage creature," she repeated to herself. But she had promised that she would stay and now she could hear her heart scolding her for breaking her word. Belle told herself that she would never have survived back

there. There was a curse on that castle. She didn't know who the beast was, or what made him behave as he did, but he certainly had an evil soul.

He did not deserve the sacrifice she would have to make. She would never have been able to live with him and those absurd talking household objects. Yes, they were polite, friendly, and thoughtful, but she could not chat with a wardrobe, confide in a teapot, and have her dinner served by a clock whose face had a moustache where its hands should be! She would have gone crazy if she had stayed!

But there was no time to think about that now! She was still in danger. How was she to get out of that terrifying forest? Would she survive the biting cold which tore at her face and hands? And what if he was following her? Finally, she summoned up the courage to look behind her. The Beast was nowhere to be seen, but what she did see was just as terrible.

A pack of wolves was drawing nearer and nearer, their yellow eyes shining threateningly through the starless night. Belle spurred on the horse, who broke

into a gallop. The wolves followed them. Food was hard to find in the snow-covered forest and they were determined not to let this opportunity pass them by.

Philippe had ventured on to a frozen lake, but his weight cracked the thin ice and Belle found herself drenched by the icy water. She prayed that they would make it safely to the other bank, and that the wolves would not dare to follow. But they had already caught up with her.

Panting breathlessly from fear and exhaustion, Philippe tried to go on, but one of the wolves slashed at him with its claws. The horse reared up, writhing in pain, and his reins became entangled in the branches of a tree. Belle was knocked to the ground. She struggled to her feet and groped around desperately for something to use as a weapon.

There was a branch poking up out of the snow. Belle grabbed it, but she was surrounded. It would be impossible to defend herself. Their mouths open, the wolves crept closer and closer to her.

Belle covered her face with her cape. She could no longer think. She had nowhere to hide; it was all over for her. But as one wolf closed in, fangs bared, ready to take her by the throat, a ferocious growl drowned out the howling of the pack.

Suddenly, the wolf yelped in pain. Belle raised her head. It was the Beast, who was shielding her with his massive body, just as he had done earlier to the rose. He was now fighting savagely against the wolves. His sharp claws were deadly, his strength monstrous, but there was something else which drove him to fight so courageously. Clinging tightly to Philippe, Belle watched, both terrified

and fascinated by the ferocious battle.
Something seemed to double the Beast's
power. He threw one of the wolves
against a tree, he beat another two down
to the ground, he injured another. The
wolves realised that nothing could defeat
the enormous creature. They began to
back off, whimpering, and disappeared
into the dense forest.

The Beast turned to Belle, his blue

eyes full of suffering. He let out a howl, grunted as he struggled to reach her, and fell to the ground, overcome with pain and fatigue. Belle considered the situation. Around them, the coast was clear; the path was deserted and the wolves had gone. The Beast did not have the strength to follow her. It was the perfect moment to escape. Belle was about to jump on Philippe again, but then she stopped.

The Beast had chosen to save her from the wolves. He had fought without fear for his own life. But why? To keep her prisoner? To terrorise her with his outbursts of anger? Or was it because he saw her as a precious treasure, like the rose, something to defend to the very death. She didn't understand why he wanted so much to see her locked up in the castle. What did he want from her? She was terribly confused. She only knew that she couldn't abandon him. The wolves would have killed her if he hadn't arrived.

She drew closer to the body which lay in the snow. It took all her strength, but somehow she managed to lift him on to the horse. Then she covered him with her cape, and they set off slowly down the road which led to the castle. She was met by the servants, who helped her, astounded by what had happened.

"The master has never behaved like this before!" exclaimed Lumiere. "He never left the castle before, for fear that someone would see him."

"Thank you for coming back," added Mrs Potts. "You will see that everything will work out, my dear!"

"I only hope that I've done the right thing!" sighed Belle. The Beast, meanwhile, was coming back to

his senses, but his injuries still needed treatment.

"Keep still. Don't do that." Belle took his paw delicately, dipped a cloth in clean water, and placed it on the wound. He moved his hand, whimpering.

"I told you to be still," she scolded.

"It hurts!" he protested.

"If you were still, it wouldn't hurt you." As she spoke, Belle realised that she was no longer afraid of the monstrous figure.

"Well, if you hadn't run away, none of this would have happened!" he said, with an offended air.

"And if you hadn't frightened me, I wouldn't have run away! Anyway, you should learn to control yourself!" she said firmly, leaving him speechless. Mrs Potts, Lumiere and Cogsworth were staring at one another in astonishment. No-one had ever spoken to the master in that way before! But Belle's voice was sweeter as she added,

"Now be still. This will sting a bit." Without thinking, she spoke from her heart. "By the way, thank you for saving my life." The Beast wasn't expecting gratitude. Taken aback by her words, he was silent for a moment. Then he spoke, and his words left Belle speechless.

"At your service!" he replied.

The Big News

Belle was no longer afraid of the Beast. She had become used to his ugliness, and he no longer seemed to be ashamed of his appearance. He had suddenly changed, and had even learned to smile! And then, one day, he told her,

"I have a surprise for you!"

He lead her down the corridor and stopped in front of a large door.

"There's something I want to show you, but you have to close your eyes."

Belle agreed, full of curiosity. When

she opened them, she found herself in the middle of an enormous room, whose walls were covered with books.

"I don't believe it," she murmured with a small voice. "I've never seen so many books in my life! It's wonderful!"

"Well, now they're all yours!" said the Beast, with a joyful smile.

"Oh, thank you, thank you!" Belle was so excited that, without thinking, she took his paw in her hand and squeezed it. Later, they had lunch together. The curtains had been raised and the room was full of light. The Beast had done everything he could to make her happy. They became friends. They

discovered the joy of being together. It was wonderful to walk in the snow-

covered park. Belle had never imagined it would be possible to joke with him, although she now often found herself doubled over with laughter. How funny he was, that big creature timidly holding out his paws to feed the little birds which flew all around them, not at all frightened of his horrible claws.

They talked for hours on end, sitting at the fireplace, illuminated only by the sparks of the fire. Belle had found some-one who understood her, someone who she could confide in. He looked at her strangely, and she felt confused when those deep blue eyes rested on her. How much kindness there was in that look!

"Belle, have you ever been in love?" he asked her. Her voice had become almost a whisper, as she replied,

"No, never, not yet."

The Beast squeezed her hand with infinite tenderness. She told him about her loneliness, her life in the village, her father and even about Gaston.

"He wants to marry me, but I could never love someone like him. He's... he's ugly inside!"

He looked at her in silence. He never spoke of himself. Only once:

"I, too, am a prisoner in this castle. I, too, am a stranger to the world!" he sighed. Belle would have liked to ask him why. Why was there a spell on the castle? And why was his human soul trapped within an animal's body? But she did not dare ask him. She understood that it was not yet time.

Little by little, Belle realised that her feelings towards the Beast were changing. Never before had anyone awakened those emotions within her. No-one had ever tried to share her hopes, her desires and her dreams, until she met the mysterious, tragic beast.

At last, they decided to celebrate their friendship with a magnificent dinner. The big day arrived. Belle admired herself happily in the mirror. The wardrobe had chosen a splendid golden gown for her, which perfectly outlined her figure. Her hair, gathered at the nape of her neck, flowed lightly down on to her shoulders.

The evening was to be a special one, and she felt excited, and a little nervous, too. He was waiting for her at the top of the stairs. He looked elegant in a blue jacket with gold buttons, his mane neatly trimmed by the scissors. He smiled at her thoughtfully. But when Belle saw his fangs, she no longer felt fear, but a great, heart-warming tenderness!

He offered her his arm and walked her to the table. A violin began to play, and the music was so sweet that Belle felt like dancing. She ran towards the Beast, took him by the hand, and led him to the centre of the hall. He was clumsy, shy and embarrassed, but his eyes glowed with happiness. Belle's eyes shone, too, like

mirrors to his. She laid her head on his chest. The truth did not scare her any more: the man of her dreams was forgotten, for she had fallen in love with the Beast!

The music came to an end and the candlelight became a dim glow. Belle and the Beast went out on to the terrace. Around them, a magical, starry sky cast its spell on the couple.

"Belle, are you happy here with me?" He had taken her hand and was holding it in his paws. She did not hesitate.

"Yes!" she replied, staring into his

eyes. But her gaze fell as a distant memory cast its shadow over her.

"What is it?" The thought of her father had disturbed the happiness of the moment.

"If only I could see my father again... I miss him so much!"

"There is a way!" The Beast seemed to be able to grant her every wish. He handed her a magic mirror, which had the power to show her anything she wished.

"I want to see my father!"

Belle cried at once. And Maurice appeared. He was searching for her in the frozen forest, but he was sick and his strength was fading.

"Father!" she cried in anguish. "He could be dying, and I'm not there!" she added, her heart aching.

"Then you must go to him!" said the Beast.

She was stunned. Was he saying that she was free? She looked into his eyes, which had become hopelessly sad. Once, she had believed that only her freedom could make her truly happy. Now, she could barely imagine her life without the Beast. It would be hard to leave him.

But she had to do it. She had to save her father. She could hear, once again, her mother's plea,

"Your father needs you, Belle. Don't ever leave him." No love, however great, could make her forget that promise. She held the mirror out to him, but he shook his head.

"Take it with you; this way you will always have a way to look back, and remember me," he whispered.

His words touched her heart. She knew that he loved her, even if he would never have the courage to admit it. Belle should have told him that she didn't care

if he was a beast, because she loved him for his gentle spirit, his compassion and his sensitivity.

"Thank you for understanding that my father needs me!" She caressed his sweet, monstrous face. She wanted to

kiss him, but instead she ran off, her eyes full of tears, without looking back. The last thing she heard, before mounting Philippe and being swallowed up by the forest, was the desperate howl of the Beast, who watched her as she left his life forever. His howl held within it all the unhappiness in the world.

THE MAGIC MIRROR

Guided by the magic mirror, Belle found her way through the dense forest. The pain in her heart was unbearable. She had abandoned the Beast and yet she did not know if she would reach her father in time! There he was! Maurice was lying on the ground, motionless. Belle approached him, trembling. He was half-frozen, but his heart was still beating.

It was sunrise by the time they reached home. Maurice had collapsed again and Belle put him to bed. Together, the warmth of the room and the loving care of his daughter helped him to regain consciousness. He opened his eyes. Maybe he was dreaming…was it really Belle?

"Everything's alright, Father. I've come back," she reassured him.

"I thought I would never see you again!" His daughter meant all the world to him. "And the Beast?"

"He ... he let me go. He's different now, Father."

There was a noise behind her. Belle turned around and saw Chip, the teacup, jump out of her bag. Her little friend, seeing Belle about to leave the castle, had decided to go with her. But there was no time for explanations. Someone was knocking on the door, and whoever it was seemed to be in a great hurry.

Janine entered, gasping for breath, as though she had run all the way there.

"I heard you had come back. They saw you. Belle, your father is in danger!"

"Janine, what are you talking about?" Belle asked impatiently, drawing her friend aside. Maurice was still weak. She didn't want to disturb him.

"They told me that one night your father went to the village tavern," Janine blurted out. "He was soaking wet, he looked desperate and he said that you were being held captive by a monstrous beast, who had locked you up in the tower of his castle. He wanted the townsmen to help him rescue you. Naturally, no-one believed him. Everyone laughed and made fun of him until two men threw him out into the snow."

"Poor Father," sighed Belle.

"But that's not all!" Janine continued. "Now they are saying that your father is crazy and the director of the asylum is coming to take him away!"

"My father is not crazy!" Belle protested. "Everything he said about the Beast is true! I was being held prisoner!" And she told her friend everything that had happened in the castle on the hill.

"You went up there? How could you be so brave?" Janine shuddered when she thought about the evil castle and the strange rumours she had heard about it.

"You know, no-one dares to go near that place. It seems to have been empty for ages, but one day Bernard, the woodsman, went hunting, got lost, and ended up right in front of the castle gates. He told everyone that he heard strange howling noises, coming from the castle. They say that it is inhabited by some ferocious animal! And you went all the way there?"

"I had to Janine, to save my father. But it wasn't so terrible."

Belle told Janine all about her adventure and about her tender feelings for that lonely and unhappy creature. She really needed to tell someone about it!

"You can't be telling me that you're in love with a monster!" Janine interrupted.

She couldn't believe it. Belle was in love with a monster, when she could have married Gaston! "You're not serious! Come on! You're crazy, as crazy as your father!" shouted the little girl, backing away from her.

Janine's tale was true, unfortunately. A rapid hammering on the door brought Belle face-to-face with a tall, thin man with a menacing air.

"I have come to take your father away," said Mr D'Arque, the director of the asylum. A crowd of curious people had come with him, and they all seemed to agree that the inventor, Maurice, was quite mad.

"My father is not crazy!" screamed

Belle. But Maurice had staggered to the door, where Le Fou was once again baiting him.

"Maurice! Tell us again, how big was the beast that you saw?"

"You wouldn't believe it! He was at least eight feet tall! No! More like nine feet!" shouted Maurice, shaken by the memory of the danger which he and Belle had faced. Everyone burst out laughing.

"Only a lunatic could come up with a story like that," chuckled Le Fou, as two big orderlies bundled the poor inventor into the carriage which would take him to the asylum. Belle fought back with all her strength.

"I will not permit you to do this!" she shouted, running about desperately. Why was no-one listening to her? Then she saw Gaston, and her hopes rose. They would believe him. He was important in the village.

The young man approached her.

"Poor Belle!" he said sympathetically, his arm around her shoulders, as if to console her.

"Gaston, help me! You know that he's not crazy!" she pleaded.

"Hmmm…" Gaston seemed to be thinking, although this was unusual for him. There was nothing pleasant about the look on his face. "Yes, I could clear up this whole misunderstanding, if—"

"If what?" Belle asked, full of hope. Maybe she had been wrong about him. Maybe he really loved her after all and would now set everything straight, would help her!

"—if you married me!" Now she understood: Gaston had been involved all along. He had called Mr D'Arque, he had spread rumours that her father was crazy, he had done it all so that he could force her into marrying him!

"Never!" she shouted, backing off with disgust. They were about to take Maurice away to the asylum. If only she could convince them that she was telling the truth. The magic mirror! Yes, she could make them all see that the Beast really existed. She ran to get it.

"Show me the monster!" she commanded the mirror. And, in front of the terrified eyes of the villagers, the mirror revealed the image of a frightening creature, his jaws open in a terrifying growl. Belle tried to explain that he wasn't dangerous, that he would not hurt anyone at all, because he was kind and gentle.

"He's my friend," she said, tenderly. Her gentle expression did not escape Gaston's notice.

76

"If I didn't know better, I might think that you were in love with that horrible monster!"

"He's not a monster, Gaston. You're the monster!" Belle shouted back. Gaston exploded with anger.

"She's just as crazy as that poor old man!" he shouted to the crowd. Then he began persuading the villagers that the Beast was a threat to the town, that he would steal their children away from them and destroy their homes.

"And I say: let's kill the Beast!" In vain, Belle tried to stop him. She tried to make him see that the Beast would never harm the village, but it was too much for Gaston's pride. If the Beast had destroyed her love for him, then he would destroy the Beast!

"If you're not with us, you're against us!" Gaston declared and ordered that Belle and her father be locked up in the cellar to stop them from warning the monster. The door closed behind them. Belle tried hopelessly to free herself, beating on the door with her fists and screaming. No-one seemed to hear her calls. Everyone was listening to Gaston. Her heart skipped a beat when she heard Gaston yell.

"We will free the town of the Beast. Who's with me?" A chorus of approval answered him.

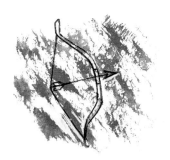

THE ATTACK ON THE CASTLE

Belle paced up and down the cellar floor in despair.

"I have to warn the Beast. This is all my fault!" She thought back to what she had seen in the magic mirror, to that anguished howl. She knew that nothing would stop Gaston's fury. He did not really care about the safety of the village; he only wanted to rid himself of that rival to his love. And there she was, trapped between four walls, just waiting, unable to do anything!

She paced nervously up and down, her soul tormented. She absolutely had to get free, but how? Not even her father could help her. All of a sudden, they heard a sputtering, followed by a tremendous noise. They ran to the window and saw Maurice's latest invention thundering towards the cellar, and heard a voice shout.

"I'm coming!" It was Chip! In all the confusion, no-one had noticed him start up the strange machine. It only took one big push to knock down the cellar door and set his friends free.

"You've saved the day!" exclaimed Belle, managing to smile again for an instant. Free at last! She mounted Philippe and took the road which led back to the enchanted castle.

"Don't let it be too late," prayed

Belle, as she spurred the horse on. Soon, they would be there.

The castle seemed deserted, blanketed

in darkness which was broken only by lightning from the storm which raged overhead. There was no sign of Gaston, nor of the Beast. Belle felt a terrible sense of foreboding. She raised her eyes towards the ramparts of the west wing.

"No!" she cried with all her might. That shout was stronger than the noise of the pounding rain, stronger than Gaston's rage, stronger than the desperation of the Beast. It was so strong that it stopped Gaston's club in mid-air as he raised it to give the Beast a final, mortal blow.

"Why doesn't he defend himself?

Why doesn't he do something to save himself?"

But Belle knew the answer. Without her, his life had no meaning and only death could free him from his torment. But now she had returned. With a ferocious burst of strength, the Beast knocked Gaston's club from his hands and turned on his aggressor. The battle had begun! Belle, running frantically, reached the terrace of the west wing just as the Beast, gripping his rival by the throat, dangled him in mid-air. If he let the young man go, Gaston would fall to his death.

"Don't do it!" Belle wanted to scream, but the words stayed unspoken. Some-how, the Beast seemed to hear her, and through his love for her, he was able to show mercy. Gaston sobbed, helpless with fear, and begged for his life. The Beast put him back on the ground.

"Get out!" he hissed. Then Belle spoke.

"I'm here." His rage dissolved and a smile appeared on the Beast's face as he turned towards Belle. He climbed up the wall to the balcony above him to reach her. He held out his arm to her.

"Belle, you came back," he whispered adoringly as he stroked her hair. She had arrived in time, and nothing could part them now. But their happiness was about to be shattered. Neither of them had seen Gaston creep towards them, a knife clenched in his fist. He ferociously stabbed the Beast in the back with all the rage and jealousy in his heart. The Beast spun around with a whimper of pain.

Startled, Gaston backed away, lost his balance, and toppled into the abyss. As he

fell, Gaston reached out to grab the Beast,
but Belle held on to him tightly, and
dragged him on to the terrace. The Beast
was lying on the ground. His breathing
was shallow as his life ebbed away.

"Maybe it's better ... better this way,"
he murmured weakly. Belle was at his
side, gently stroking him. It was as

though she was trying to give him back the will to live through her touch. The tears which had filled her eyes now flowed unchecked down her cheeks. She didn't think that she could take much more. Everything that had happened had been caused by stupidity and ignorance and Gaston's wretched pride.

"Don't speak like that," she said, trying to steady her voice. "Now we are together, everything will be all right." What an incredible lie! With every second that passed, life was flowing out of that big, hairy body, and the light was fading from those blue eyes which she had learned to love.

Her only true love was dying, leaving her alone. Once again, she would be alone with only her father for company. Yes, he was kind, but he was as fragile as a crystal glass. Instead of defending her, he needed to be protected. She would be alone, with

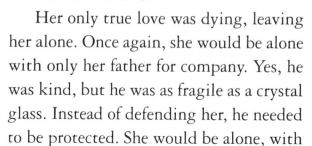

no hope of escaping from the town where the people would have nothing to do with her, where life wasn't worth living.

"At least I was able to see you one last time." The Beast used all his

strength to raise a paw and caress the face which he loved so much, and somehow found the energy to smile. Then his arm fell back and his eyelids covered those blue, blue irises forever.

"No, no!" sobbed Belle, her head

buried in his chest. "I beg you, don't leave me! Please, don't leave me!" She could not bear to be without him, because ... because...

"I love you!" she whispered at last. And that was the truth.

It was so clear, as clear as the sky on a beautiful summer's day, this truth which had always been there for all to see; and yet only now was Belle able to see it for herself. A few steps away from them, the last rose petal fell. Belle did not notice.

Nor would she have even cared. All was still. Even her heart seemed to have stopped. And at that moment, the Beast's heart stopped beating.

THE SPELL IS BROKEN

A flash of light surrounded the dying Beast. Belle raised her head and saw his enormous body being lifted up in a spiral. An irresistible force was at work: first the fur disappeared, then his claws. Hands appeared, then feet. What was happening?

No more mane, no more fangs – and there, before Belle's wide, frightened eyes, stood a handsome young man.

"Belle, it's me!" He came close to her and caressed her hair, as tenderly as ever.

His voice was the same, although clearer and more vibrant. Belle looked at him, hesitating.

She looked into his eyes: blue, intense, tender. They were the eyes she had seen in the portrait in the west wing, the eyes which had stared at her with rage, with disbelief, with hope, with despair and with love. When she looked into those eyes, she knew that she still loved him.

"It's really you." And finally, they kissed! A golden light bathed them as they embraced. Then the magic began. The golden glow flowed away, skimming around the castle, transforming it into a

glorious palace once more. Looking around, Belle and the young prince found themselves surrounded by their friends from the castle, who had become human again. Lumiere, Cogsworth, Mrs Potts, Chip and all the others, had been changed back into real people because of the strength of their love.

Later they sat down to a feast. Belle wore her gold dress, while her prince wore the blue jacket with gold buttons. They sat at the table. Cogsworth served the dinner, while the violin played their song. The prince could now open his heart and reveal to Belle his life's secret.

"I had everything: youth, good looks, wealth and power. But I was terribly cold and self-centred. One dark evening, an old woman appeared at the castle, asking

for lodging for the night. In exchange, she offered me a rose. Accustomed as I was to being surrounded only by beautiful things, I couldn't bear the sight of that sad, old woman. I was horrible and tried to chase her off. But, to my horror, the beggar disappeared and in her place was a beautiful fairy, her eyes full of rage. It was then that I understood, but it was too late. The fairy cast a spell on the castle and turned me into a horrible beast because my heart was cruel and loveless.

"I would be only able to return to my human form again if, by my twenty-first birthday and before the rose lost its last petal, I had learned to love and was able to make someone love me. She left me the magic mirror as my only window to the world, the world which my own cruelty had taken from me."

The prince lowered his gaze, reliving the pain of that moment. Belle understood now. She thought of the desperation which she had seen in his eyes, of his sudden and terrible bursts of anger.

"I thought I would stay like that forever. Who could ever have loved a beast?" the prince continued. "Then you arrived, and I loved you from the beginning. You were more than I had ever dreamed of. It was a miracle. You fell in love with me – with a frightening beast.

You saved me!"

"I could see your beauty, the beauty of your soul, because I saw you through my heart's eyes," replied Belle. Then she rose and, just as she had done on that other night, led him to the centre of the hall. They danced a long, romantic waltz.

The adventure had ended. Belle had finally found the man of her dreams. But she still had one last desire. Now she wanted to write a book.

"I will tell my story," she confided to her prince. "The most incredible, fascinating, and magical of all love stories…"

A SELECTION OF ACTION/ADVENTURE TITLES

AVAILABLE FROM BANTAM YOUNG ADULT BOOKS

PRICES SHOWN BELOW WERE CORRECT AT THE TIME OF GOING
TO PRESS. HOWEVER TRANSWORLD PUBLISHERS RESERVE THE
RIGHT TO SHOW NEW RETAIL PRICES ON COVERS WHICH MAY
DIFFER FROM THOSE PREVIOUSLY ADVERTISED IN THE TEXT
OR ELSEWHERE.

0 553 40705 8	**MARCUS MUSTARD**	*J H Brennan*	£2.99
0 553 40655 8	**WORLD OF THE STIKS**	*Douglas Hill*	£2.99
0 553 40656 6	**THE ELECTRIC KID**	*Garry Kilworth*	£2.99
0 553 50327 8	**CYBERCATS**	*Garry Kilworth*	£3.50
0 553 40802 X	**WHITE OUT**	*Anthony Masters*	£2.99
0 553 40522 5	**HELL ON EARTH**	*Anthony Masters*	£2.99

Don't miss the second title in the *Cade* trilogy,
coming soon from Bantam Books . . .

CADE
THE MOONS OF LANNAMUR
by Douglas Hill

*The Occian Senior Controller's eyelids rose and fell.
He leaned forward, baring his teeth. 'Let it be clearly
understood . . . Whoever finds the thief, whatever
else they do, they* must not leave Cade alive!'

Cade heads impatiently for the far-off world of
Lannamur and its two colonized moons, in search
of a Fsefsety – a gentle insectile alien – who holds
priceless information locked into his memory . . .

It should be easy. But the fanatical Purity Defend-
ers on Lannamur and interference from the
Commonwealth Intelligence Agency are just the
first problems facing Cade. For waiting for him and
his companion, combat-act Raishe, to reach the
moons is the mysterious K'liev – a cold-eyed robot-
ics expert whose past is as hidden as his face. And
behind Cade, following his every move, is a squad of
murderous Occians . . .

The second title in an action-packed trilogy that
follows the tricky, trouble-making Cade on a
planet-hopping escapade around the galaxy.

0 553 50330 8